L 4.0
P. 005

Riptide

by Frances Ward Weller / illustrated by Robert J. Blake

PaperStar

The Putnam & Grosset Group

For Frank, my Rip in man's clothing. —F.W.W.

For Fido, my very special dog. —R.J.B.

Zachary lived in a Cape Cod house which had pine woods for a comforter and shingles bleached to driftwood by the sea. It was only a salt marsh and three sand dunes from the great ocean beach, but a long way from the village. So Zachary wished he had a dog for company.

A cuddly pup that licked was what he wanted. His father brought a golden ball of fur, as warm and soft as Zachary's dream. "He needs a hug," Zach's father said, "and then he needs a name."

They called him Rip. Riptide Windjammer. Not Scout or Pal or any of the plain old names for dogs they knew. Riptide for a current that runs out to sea when sandbars crumble. Windjammer for a ship that runs before the wind.

They didn't know he'd live up to his name.

They didn't know the sea would call to Rip, as it calls fishermen and sailors, surfers and sunbathers. The ocean always drummed Pied Piper songs for Zach's dog Rip.

For just one summer Riptide followed Zach's small surfboard and learned the tricky ways of currents racing round the sandbars. But by September he was off on business of his own. All day he'd run for miles along the beach, and then swim back as many miles to where the path for home began.

"He wants to be a dolphin," Zachary's father said. "See how he dives into a long-haired wave, comes up and dives again."

But Zachary thought, Rip wants to be the wind. He's like the wind, the way he races down the shore and rides the sea.

Zach still wished Rip would lick, and guard the applestand in fall, and chase his whiffleballs in spring. Instead, year-round Riptide patrolled the beach, even when ice piled up along the sand and only huddled gulls were there to see him running by.

And worst of all was summer, when Rip wanted more than running free to be a picknicker, a surfer, even a lifeguard, herding toddlers in the shallows just like a sheepdog with new lambs.

Rip couldn't read the big clear sign that said NO DOGS ON NAUSET BEACH. So when the beach patrol went after him with whistles and their walkie-talkies, Rip thought there surely must be some mistake. At first he simply paid them no attention. And then he learned a dozen new escapes.

The gray-haired tower of a man who wore a badge and nameplate, "Nick," had eyes that swept the beach and didn't miss a thing. "I'll chase that rascal from here to Halifax, if I have to!" Zach heard him tell the lifeguards.

Rip wasn't very old when Zach was called one day to fetch him, and found him giving a small boy a ride. The child let Rip's tail go and splashed toward deeper water. Rip spun and leaped beyond him, barking warnings.

"You hear that ruckus, son?" Nick frowned at Zachary. "Your Rip-tide seems to think he has to guard this beach. We've eighteen guards already! Keep him home!"

And so they tried.

Zach's father took him to the barbershop, where conversation crackled and there were pats aplenty. But Rip looked bored and moaned beside the door.

Zach and his mother popped Rip in their truck and drove to Halifax for corn and let the wind whip his ears out like flags. He's just pretending it's the beach, thought Zachary. No sooner was the corn heaped on the stand than Rip was gone again.

There never was a doubt the beach was where they'd find him. The phone calls kept repeating, "Come get Rip." And on the beach Rip led his chasers first one way and then another. He swam and ran and mooched and ran, made friends and ran. When chasers came too close, he swam to sea and down the beach for home.

Just like the wind he never could be caught.

As summer followed summer, Nick seemed to watch Rip with a growing twinkle in his eyes. And everyone began to feel that Rip belonged.

Then came an August day when Zachary headed for the beach. The week's first sunshine warmed the footbridge through the marsh. Zach's bare feet thudded on the boards. Boom! Boom! echoed the waves, still drumming from a storm. Somewhere far off a gull or siren cried.

Zach wondered where Rip was, this shiny day. And then a flock of sirens wailed beyond the dunes, and Zach began to run.

The beach was not its usual merry sprawl. Tense knots of people hovered at the water's edge. Lifeguards charged through the surf with ropes and boards and buoys to reach a chain of swimmers drifting out to sea.

It was a real riptide, caused by the passing storm. And where was Rip?

Zach spied him standing at attention, gazing out to sea. Then Riptide ran down the dune and bolted for an open stretch of swells.

"No, Rip!" yelled Zachary. "Come back!"

Instead Rip burst into the water, battling waves that buried him and tried to drive him back. Riptide Windjammer had a mission of his own.

Beyond him Zachary saw a single head. Rip circled, and two hands that beckoned reached to grab his tail. Zachary stood breathless at the water's edge. And Rip, towing the girl behind him, swam for shore the way he always did, with no mistake.

Zach sloshed in ankle deep, but Nick waded out beyond him and snatched up the girl before a wave's curl caught her.

"It seems," he called to Zachary as he carried her to shore, "your rascal Rip has saved a life!"

But then a waterfall of wave cascaded down on Rip. He clawed for footing in the shallows, but backwash dragged him out into the undertow.

"Oh no!" Zach yelled. "He's sliding toward the rip! Can't someone get him?"

It seemed Rip paddled with a purpose, but he was being carried out to sea. For as he struck the seabound current he sailed out still faster, like a gull upon the wind.

"Turn!" Zach shouted.

But Rip sailed out till Zach could barely tell his dog from sky and water.

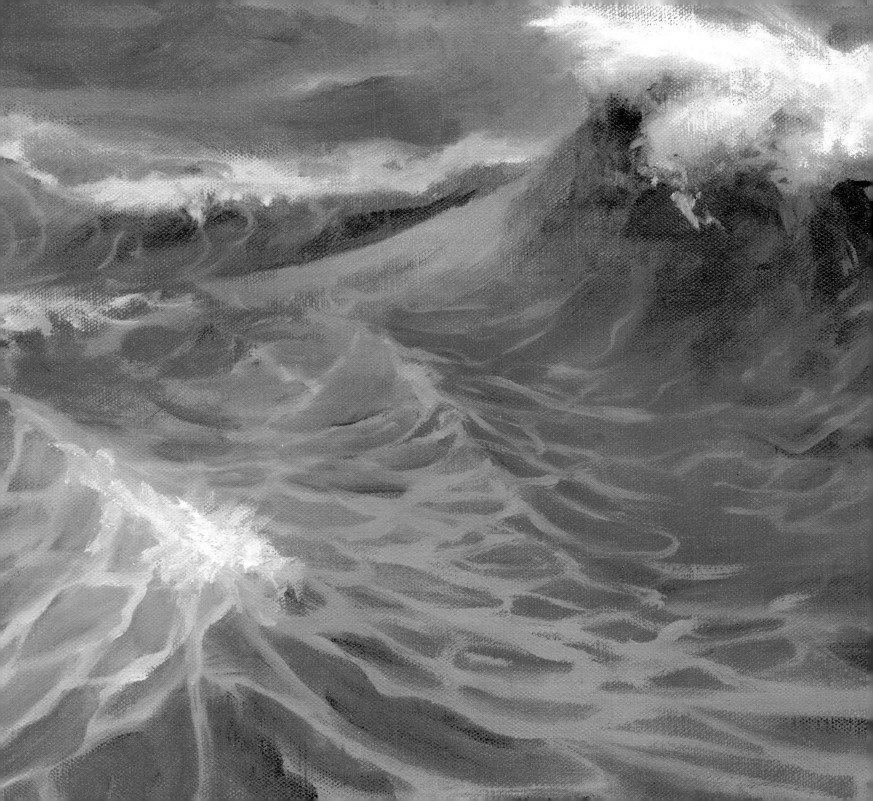

"He doesn't seem scared," murmured Zach.

"That is his world," Nick said. And swinging up his binoculars, he gave a cheer. "All right! He's veering, swimming down the beach!" Then pushing back his cap, Nick chuckled and shook his head. "Looks like he really is my nineteenth guard," he said.

So for the thousandth time Rip swam for home. Zach strained to watch him in the dazzle of the sea. Then Zach began to run. He'd meet Rip down the beach and walk him home.

The beach patrol never chased Rip again. The lifeguards let him join their drills, and as he aged they drove him home for supper. And Zachary was content when Rip dug canyons at the ocean's edge, ran windsprints with the guards and rode out to the end of land in Nick's old jeep.

For now Zach knew what Rip had always known. Rip was the nineteenth guard, as restless and as constant as the wind. His place was on the beach.

There wouldn't ever be another like him.

I am indebted to Arthur, Meredith and Ronald Fancy of East Orleans for wonderful, funny, bittersweet tales of their beloved pet. I was fortunate, too, to share the memories of Jerre Austin, former head lifeguard at Nauset, and Paul Fulcher, Orleans Park Superintendent—who when Rip died told the local newspaper, "He was my nineteenth lifeguard." It was this obituary that first inspired this book.

I hope Rip's story also honors the late Jim Nickerson, longtime director of the Nauset Beach Patrol, and all the unnamed guards who brave the wiles of the Atlantic along Cape Cod's great outer beach.

Printed on recycled paper

Text copyright © 1990 by Frances Ward Weller.
Illustrations copyright © 1990 by Robert J. Blake.
All rights reserved. This book, or parts thereof, may not be reproduced in any form without permission in writing from the publisher. A PaperStar Book, published in 1996 by The Putnam & Grosset Group, 200 Madison Avenue, New York, NY 10016. PaperStar is a registered trademark of The Putnam Berkley Group, Inc. The PaperStar logo is a trademark of The Putnam Berkley Group, Inc. Originally published in 1990 by Philomel Books, New York. Published simultaneously in Canada. Printed in the United States of America. Library of Congress Cataloging-in-Publication Data

Weller, Frances Ward.
Riptide / by Frances Ward Weller; illustrated by Robert J. Blake.   p.   cm.
Summary: Zach's dog Riptide loves the sea and proves himself worthy of being the nineteenth lifeguard on Cape Cod's Nauset Beach.
[1. Dogs—Fiction.   2. Cape Cod (Mass.)—Fiction.]   I. Blake, Robert J., ill.
II. Title.   PZ7.W454Ri   1990   [Fic]—dc20   89-8527   CIP   AC

ISBN 0-698-11386-1
3   5   7   9   10   8   6   4   2